UNCHARTED
TERRITORY

Harry, the Happy Snake of Happy Hollow

Harry, the Happy Snake of Happy Hollow

Join Harry, the gentle snake, and his woodland friends
on their merry misadventures.

Library of Congress Cataloging-in-Publication Data

Birchmore, Daniel A. 1951-

Harry the Happy Snake of Happy Hollow / written by Daniel A. Birchmore;
illustrated by Gail E. Lucas
p. cm.

Summary: Awakening from his long winter's nap to find the other animals busily working at their own special tasks,
Harry the snake searches for his own work and discovers adventures along the way.

ISBN 1-887813-08-X (book & audio: alk. paper)
ISBN 1-887813-06-3 (book only: alk. paper)
ISBN 1-887813-07-1 (audio)

[1. Snakes – Fiction. 2. Animals – Fiction.]
I. Lucas, Gail, 1937- ill. II. Title.
III. Series: Birchmore, Daniel A., 1951-
Adventures of Harry the Happy Snake of Happy Hollow.

PZ7.B51179Har 1996
[E]--dc20

96-4227
CIP AC

Layout and Design by Becca Hutchinson

David C. Lock, Publisher

Printed in Korea
Published in the United States by Cucumber Island Storytellers
P.O. Box 920
Montchanin, DE 19710

Please visit our site on the World Wide Web.
http://www.cucumberisland.com

Harry, the Happy Snake of Happy Hollow

Written by Daniel A. Birchmore

Illustrated by Gail Lucas

Montchanin, Delaware

PREFACE

This summer, my mother and father found a shed snakeskin in the woodpile behind their house at Happy Hollow. What a wonderful place for a snake, with a garden to explore, and walls to climb, and woods to hide in, and warm sunny spots to nap in, and chipmunks and mockingbirds and crickets to talk with. So I'm sure that's what Harry the snake does all day. What a wonderful life that must be!

Danny Birchmore
Athens, Georgia

Harry wriggled with delight as he nosed through the soft, warm loam.

"Oh, boy!" he said to himself, "I'm going to lie here part of the day in the sun and get nice and warm, and then I'll go exploring through the garden. And then maybe I'll take a nap!"

Harry lay quite still with the sun warming his smooth grey scales. "After that long cold winter it surely is nice to feel the sun again!" he thought.

Harry could hear the earthworms digging in the soil beneath him. They were humming as they dug. Each earthworm hummed a different hymn. Some hummed "Hi," some hummed "Wee," and some hummed "O."

He could hear the ants scurrying to and fro, and off in the distance he heard the rhythmic purring of a caterpillar gliding along the base of a tree.

"Everybody surely is busy today," he thought.

"Crunch!" went something. "Crunch!" it went again.
"What on earth is that?" wondered Harry. He couldn't
remember *ever* having heard that pitch of a crunch before.
"Crunch!"

Harry decided to investigate. He cautiously wriggled forward
through the leaves and grass, gliding quietly towards the
blackberry bush that grew in the open patch between the hickory
tree and the clearing.

There was nothing there but a round brown rock.
"Why, there's nothing here but a round brown rock," thought Harry.

Then he saw the rock move!
"Oh, my!" thought Harry, "I've never seen a moving rock before!"
Then he saw a long brown neck reach out from behind the rock,
and he heard a "Crunch!" as a blackberry disappeared from the
blackberry bush.

"What on earth is that?" wondered Harry.
From the safety of the bush he peered at the rock.
It didn't move.

So, Harry lay there, and he waited, and he waited, and he waited
to see what would happen next. Harry waited *so* long that he
started getting sleepy.
He grew sleepier and sleepier and sleepier, and finally Harry
grew so sleepy, that he went to sleep.

When Harry awoke, the sun was shining, and *every*body was busy gathering food. The mice were gathering grain, the birds were gathering seeds, and the chipmunks were gathering nuts. Harry yawned and stretched, and then he stretched and yawned. "You're such a lazy creature!" said the ants, shaking their antennae at Harry; "Why don't you work like the rest of us?" "What is work?" asked Harry, for he really didn't know.

"Work is carrying bits of dirt on your shoulders
to make a home," answered the ants.

Harry decided that that must be a very wise thing to do since
the ants were so busy doing it. He tried putting bits of dirt
on *his* shoulders, but because poor Harry *had* no shoulders,
the dirt kept sliding off his back.

"You silly snake!" said the ants,
"*You* can't work. You don't know how."

Poor Harry! He was *so* disappointed.

He didn't know how to work,
and he just couldn't understand
what was so important about work.

So he curled up and went to sleep.

When Harry awoke the
mockingbird was mocking him.

"Look at that lazy snake sleeping in the sun!" sang the bird.

"He can't work, and he doesn't know *how* to work!"

"The ants told me that work is carrying bits of dirt on
my shoulders, but I *have* no shoulders," said Harry.

"Silly snake! Work is gathering bugs and worms," sang the bird.

So Harry gathered bugs and worms and put them into neat
piles. But every pile quickly disappeared, and he had nothing
to show for his efforts.

And so he went to sleep.

When Harry awoke, the chipmunk was chirping at him.

"Look at that lazy snake!" chirped the chipmunk;
"He doesn't know how to work!"

"The mockingbird told me to gather bugs and worms,
but they all disappeared," said Harry.

"Silly snake! Work is gathering nuts and putting them down this hole in this tree," chirped the chipmunk.

So Harry gathered nuts
and dropped them d$_{o_{w_n}}$
the hole in the tree.

"What do we do with the nuts now?" asked Harry.
    "*I eat* them, silly snake!" chirped the chipmunk.

Poor Harry! He didn't know how to work
or why to work or when to work.

So he lay down and went to sleep.

When Harry awoke, there was a beautiful long creature with long grey scales gazing at him.

"I've never seen *anyone* able to sleep *that* long!" said the creature.

Harry felt *so* proud.

"Who are you?" asked Harry.

"I'm Sally, the she-snake," said she.

And Harry was *so* happy that he went right back to sleep.

When Harry awoke he decided it was time to explore the garden.

So he wriggled through the clover,
  and down the grassy bank,
    and up and over the rock wall that led to the garden.

"Whee!" cried Harry happily as he nudged a ripe tomato and watched it swing to and fro on the vine. He saw ripe tomatoes, and he saw ripe okra, and he saw ripe beans, and he saw ripe corn, and he saw ripe pickles!

The lady who lived by the garden was whistling as she worked.

"Oh! Oh! Oh!" she cried when she saw Harry.

"Oh!" thought Harry happily, "the lady is so excited to see me!"

Harry went on through the garden and back into the woods.

"Oh, my!" thought Harry, "what a long, happy morning this has been!" And then he found a nice shady spot to take a nap and went to sleep.

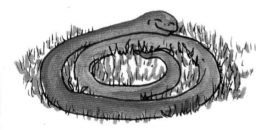

Harry and the Mouse

When Harry awoke, he stretched and yawned, and then he yawned and stretched.

"Oh, what a wonderful nap that was!" he sighed.

"I think I'll go and visit my friends at the barn."

Harry loved to visit his friends the horses and the cows and the sheep and the goats and the chickens and Penny the pig.

So,

He slⁱth_er^ed through the thickets,

And he *g l i d e d* through the grass,

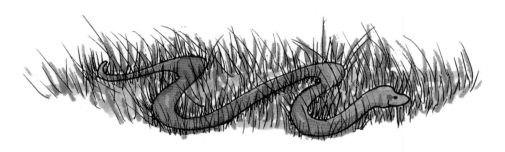

And he *hurried* d_o_w_n the creekbank

Until at last...

...he reached the barn.

"Hello, Mr. Horse," said Harry politely.
"Neigh!" said the horse.
And the horse was *so* excited to see Harry
that he jumped over the barnyard fence!

"Hello, Mrs. Cow," said Harry.
"Moo!" said the cow, and she was so excited to see
Harry that *she* jumped over the barnyard fence.

"Hello, Mr. Goat," and "Hello, Mr. Sheep,"
and "Hello, Mrs. Chicken," said Harry.
And the goat went "Baa!"
And the sheep went "Baa!"
And the chicken went "Cluck, Cluck, Cluck!" And they were all
so excited to see Harry that *they* jumped over the barnyard fence!

"Hello, Penny," said Harry.
And Penny the pig was so excited to see Harry that she wiggled
her short cute curly little tail and went right to sleep!
But then Harry had no one left to talk with.

"I think I'll go explore the barn!" said Harry. So,

He climbed on the rafters,

And he looked in the stalls,

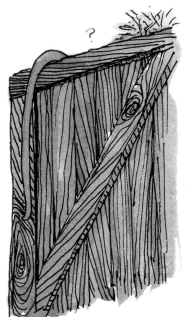

And he played in the haystack,

And he peeked over walls,

Until all of a sudden somebody said "BOO!"

Poor Harry was so frightened that he almost turned *green*!

"Oh! Oh! Oh!" cried Harry, and when he was finally brave enough to open his eyes again, he saw a small brown creature with a long pointed nose peering down at him from the rafters.

"Who are you?"
asked Harry, for he had
never seen a mouse before.

"I'm Manfred the Mouse,"
said the creature,
"and this is *my* barn!"

"Yes, sir," said Harry.

"And what do you think you're doing in *my* barn?" asked the mouse in a stern voice.

"I was just playing, sir," said Harry.

"Don't you know you have to have permission from *me* to play in *my* barn?" said the mouse.

"No, sir; I'm sorry. I didn't know!" replied Harry timidly.

Then the mouse jumped down from the rafters, and he whipped his long tail back and forth in front of Harry's nose.

"My, sir, what a long tail you have!" said Harry.

"All the better to *beat* you with!" exclaimed the mouse. And then the mouse showed Harry his long curved teeth.

"And what long teeth you have!" said Harry.

"All the better to *eat* you with!" exclaimed the mouse.

"Oh, my!" cried poor Harry, and he was so frightened that he hurried out of the barn as fast as he could, and he ran and hid behind Penny the pig.

The mockingbird was watching
and sang this little song,

"Silly, silly snake
    Can't tell a fake
        Mouse in a huff
            Showing a bluff!"

But Harry was so glad to have escaped from
that terrible mouse that he hid behind Penny
for a long, long time. Penny was sound asleep
and was snoring so softly that Harry grew
sleepy. He grew sleepier and sleepier
and sleepier; and finally Harry grew
so sleepy, that he went to sleep!

Harry and the Dog

Harry slept and slept in the warm sunshine,
and as he slept, he heard someone go

"Sniff!"

Now, everyone goes "Sniff" sometimes.

Mice do when they find cheese,
hummingbirds do when they see flowers,
and you and I do when we hear fresh
cookies baking.

But Harry had never heard anyone sniff quite
like that before.

"Sniff!"

Harry sleepily opened one eye to see who had gone "Sniff!" and he was amazed to see a creature with a long nose and a long wet tongue sniffing at his tail!

"Hello," said Harry; "who are you?"

"I'm Wooster," replied Wooster. "Who are you?"

"I'm Harry," replied Harry.

"What sort of creature are you?" asked Wooster, for he had never seen a snake before.

"What do you mean?" asked Harry.

"Are you a bird?" asked Wooster.

"I don't think so," replied Harry, "for I can't fly."

"Are you a fish?" asked Wooster.

"I don't think so," replied Harry.

"Then what are you?" asked Wooster.

"I'm *me!*" replied Harry happily.

"Oh!" said Wooster; "would you like to help me hunt for turtles?"

"Oh, yes!" exclaimed Harry; "that sounds like great fun! What shall we do when we find them?"

"We'll ask them to come out and play!" replied Wooster.

So, Harry and Wooster set out to hunt for turtles.

They hunted in the thicket,

And they asked Mr. Frog,

And they searched
in the meadow,

And they looked 'neath the log,

But they couldn't find any turtles.

"*I know!*" said Harry happily;
"Let's go ask the mockingbird; he knows *everything!*"

So, they searched in the meadow,

And they looked 'neath the log,

And they hunted in the thicket,

And they finally found
the mockingbird
in the *tree*.

"Please, Mr. Mockingbird," asked Harry,
"can you tell us where to find turtles?"

"Silly snake!" sang the mockingbird;
"You're the silliest snake I ever did see!
Turtles live inside of rocks."

So, Harry and Wooster set off to find rocks.
"I know where there are *lots* of rocks!" said Harry proudly.

So, Harry and Wooster went down to the rock wall
by the garden.

"Is anybody home?" asked Harry and Wooster.

"No!" said the crickets who lived in the wall.

"No!" said the mice who lived under the wall.

"No!" said the cat who slept on top of the wall.

"Oh," said Harry and Wooster sadly,
and they sat down beside a round brown rock.

"Yawn!" said Harry, "I'm getting sleepy."

"I am, too," said Wooster.

So, they both lay down and took a nice long nap.

When Harry and Wooster awoke, the round brown rock
was gone!

"I wonder what happened to the round brown rock?"
wondered Harry.

"Let's go hunt for frogs!" suggested Wooster.

That sounded like a wonderful idea to Harry.

So, they set off to find Mr. Frog.

They peeked in the bushes,

And they peered in the tree,

And they went in the barn,
and they looked in nearly
every place they could think of;

and they finally found Mr. Frog by the pond.

"Will you play with us?" asked Harry.

"Of course!" said Mr. Frog enthusiastically.
"Let's play follow-the-leader; I'm first!"

"Oh, what fun!" exclaimed Harry and Wooster.

So, Mr. Frog climbed down the bank,
and so did Harry and Wooster.

Then Mr. Frog jumped onto the log,
and so did Harry and Wooster.

And then Mr. Frog jumped onto the green lily pad.

"Whee!" cried Harry
as he jumped onto
the green lily pad.

"Whee!" cried Wooster as
he jumped onto the green
lily pad.

But when Wooster landed on the
green lily pad, guess what happened!

It went "Smush!"
and Down went the frog
and Down went Harry,
and Down went Wooster

To the bottom of the pond,
and they all got soaking wet!

And then Harry and Wooster

climbed out onto
　　　　　the bank.

Wooster found a nice muddy spot
　　　　　　　　　　　　　and *rolled*
　　　　　　　　　　　　　　　and *rolled*
　　　　　　　　　　　　　　　　and *rolled*
　　　　　　　　　　　　　over and
　　　　　　　　　　　　　　　over and
　　　　　　　　　　　　　　　　over, and
then he hurried home to show the lady
who lived with him his new mud coat!

And Harry was so happy after all his exciting adventures
that he s t r e t c h e d out in a warm, sunny spot
and took a nice long nap!